WHY ARE YOU SHY?

by Paul M. Kramer

PUBLISHERS
Books & Stories by Paul M. Kramer

WHY ARE YOU SHY? by Paul M. Kramer

© Paul M. Kramer October 2014. All Rights Reserved.

Aloha Publishers LLC
848 North Rainbow Boulevard, #4738
Las Vegas, NV 89107
www.alohapublishers.com

Inquiries, comments or further information are available at, www. alohapublishers.com.

Illustrations by Helga Tacke helgatacke@yahoo.com
Audio by Charly Espina Takahama charly@pmghawaii.com
Collaborator, Co-Editor, Cynthia Kress Kramer

ISBN 13 (EAN): 978-1-941095-10-2
Library of Congress Control Number (LCCN): 2014945486
Printed in Guangzhou, China. Production date: September 2014 Cohort: Batch 1

WHY ARE YOU SHY?

by Paul M. Kramer

Aloha

PUBLISHERS
Books & Stories by Paul M. Kramer

This is a story about a girl named Mary Lou.

She looked down or looked away when spoken to.

She was bashful and extremely shy.

It was hard for Mary Lou to look anyone in the eye.

Mary Lou became noticeably shy shortly after turning three.

She is now ten years old and comes from a loving family.

Mary Lou's best friend is also ten and her name is Margo.

Both girls were born and raised just outside the city of Chicago.

Mary Lou found it hard to make friends and was afraid to try.

No one truly knew why Mary Lou had become so shy.

Was she terrified of being laughed at or saying something in the wrong way?

Being so shy prevented Mary Lou from expressing herself and saying what she really wanted to say.

Mary Lou never raised her hand in class and sat silently in her chair.

She tried not to be noticed as she hid behind her hair.

Her friend Margo got invited to many parties and Mary Lou did not.

Being so shy and only having one friend, Mary Lou missed out on a lot.

Mary Lou and Margo were in the same grade.
It's hard to believe that Margo was the only friend Mary Lou ever made.
Mary Lou's bedroom was where she felt comfortable and calm.
It was where she knew she was safe and protected from harm.

Mary Lou's mom was also shy and didn't want Mary Lou to suffer anymore than she had to.

Shyness is a problem that so many children and adults go through.

As a family, they discussed the different things that they could possibly do.

They practiced shaking hands as one would say, "Hi, how are you"?

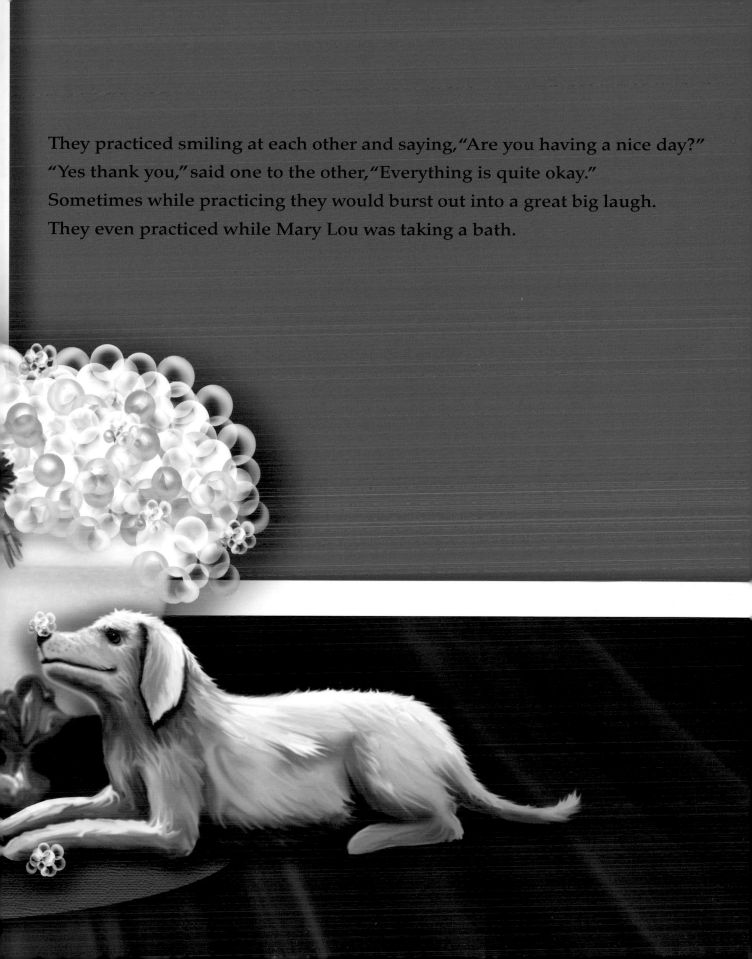

They practiced smiling at each other and saying, "Are you having a nice day?"
"Yes thank you," said one to the other, "Everything is quite okay."
Sometimes while practicing they would burst out into a great big laugh.
They even practiced while Mary Lou was taking a bath.

They took turns buying small items, as they looked the cashier in the eye.

After about three weeks of this, they noticed they weren't nearly as shy.

They learned an important lesson that being less than perfect is all right.

Being a perfectionist is not always good, especially if it causes anxiety and makes you uptight.

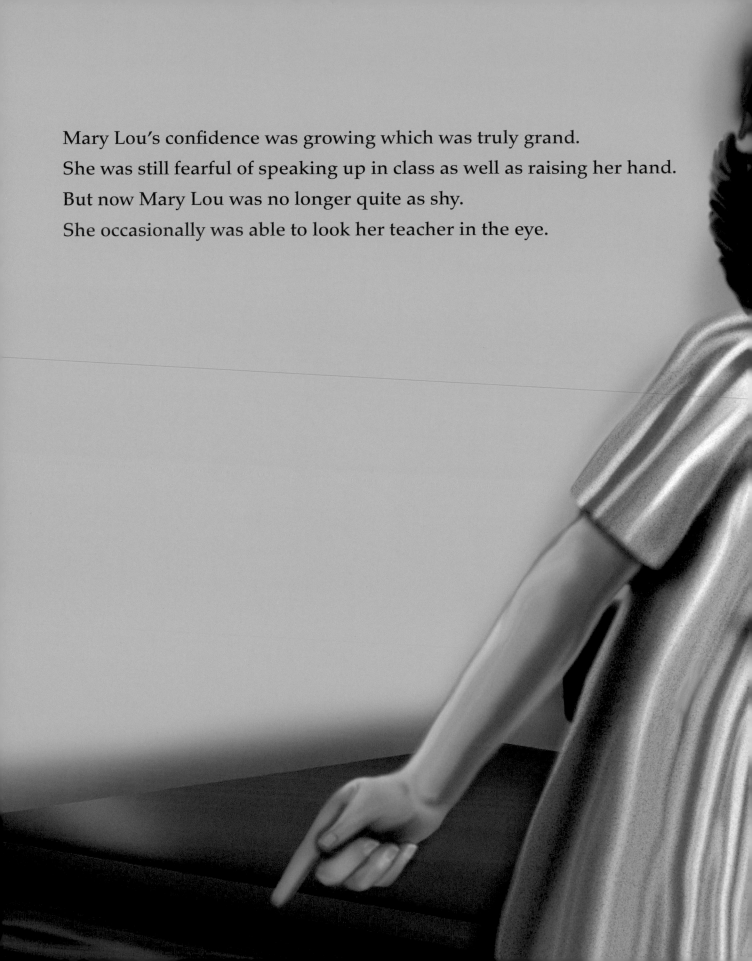

Mary Lou's confidence was growing which was truly grand.
She was still fearful of speaking up in class as well as raising her hand.
But now Mary Lou was no longer quite as shy.
She occasionally was able to look her teacher in the eye.

Mary Lou was so much happier now that she was less shy.

Her entire life was changing for the better right before her eyes.

The family agreed this new learning experience was really great.

They all decided to go out to eat and celebrate.

Mary Lou was blessed by having a beautiful sounding voice.

When asked what she wanted to do when she grew up, being a singer was her first choice.

Despite her shyness, Mary Lou was determined to take a singing lesson or even a few.

She hoped that one day she'd sing in public, which would be a dream come true.

Mary Lou's family became closer than they had ever been before.

They were grateful for what they had learned and hoped to learn more.

Mary Lou's singing teacher told her that with training she could go very far.

Her teacher said that maybe in a few years she could even become a star.

You should always try to do the best that you can do.

No one including yourself should ever expect anything more from you.

Raising your hand when you know the answer is a good first step.

Even if what you say isn't perfect, the more you try the easier it will get.

Lots of people have problems they need to overcome.
It's very difficult for most people, but easier for some.
With each baby step that you take, you'll be a little less shy.
It's only a matter of time before you can look anyone in the eye.

BORN NAKED AND EQUAL

You are not any better than anyone else.
No one else is any better than you.
You have the right to be who you are.
You are worthy and deserving in all that you do.

You need never be ashamed.
You were chosen by the process of birth.
You are not inferior to anyone.
Naked and equal everyone entered this earth.

Some had less fortunate beginnings.
Some had more challenges than others.
Many had to overcome constant obstacles.
Many grew up without fathers or mothers.

We are all children of the universe.
Our existence we need not justify.
Be not afraid to stand straight and tall,
then look everyone right in the eye.

Paul M. Kramer

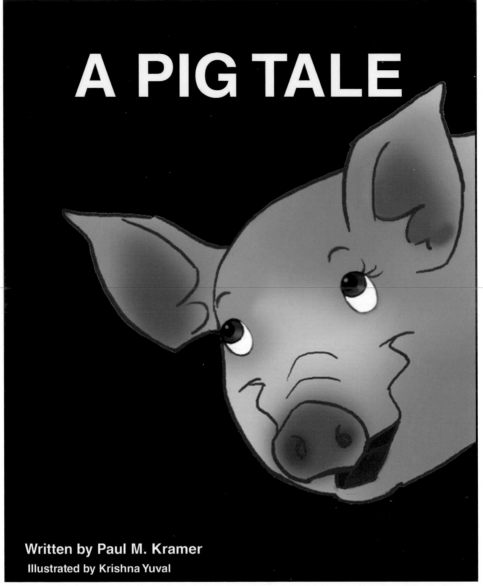

A PIG TALE

Written by Paul M. Kramer
Illustrated by Krishna Yuval

"A Pig Tale" is a sweet and touching story about a pig named Millie who was allergic to dirt and dust, and Emily, a little girl who desperately needed a friend to help ease the pain of the passing of the family dog. The moment Emily saw Millie and Millie saw Emily there was an instant and magical connection between them. They played together, took walks together and immediately became best friends. This super clean pig was so loving and gentle that the farmer and his wife allowed Millie to move into the family's house, which was a dream come true for both Emily and Millie.

ISBN: 978-1-941095-13-3, retail price: $15.95, size: 8" x 10"

It's normal and natural for people to worry from time to time. Worrying too much and too often is unnatural. How can worry benefit you if what you were worrying about doesn't happen? How can worry benefit you if what you're worrying about actually does happen? It is normal to be concerned, but excessive worry doesn't resolve anything. Have faith that you and your family will do whatever needs to be done if something you are worrying about happens.

ISBN: 978-1-941095-12-6, retail price: $15.95, size: 8" x 10"

About the Author

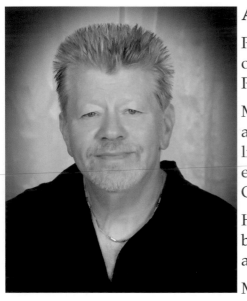

Paul M. Kramer lives in Hawaii on the beautiful island of Maui with his wife Cindy and their son Lukas. Paul was born and raised in New York City.

Mr. Kramer's books attempt to reduce stress and anxiety and resolve important issues children face in their everyday lives. His books are often written in rhyme. They are entertaining, inspirational, educational and easy to read. One of his goals is to increase the child's sense of self worth.

He has written books on various subjects such as bullying, divorce, sleep deprivation, worrying, shyness, and weight issues.

Mr. Kramer has appeared on "Good Morning America," "The Doctors," "CNN Live" as well as several other Television Shows in the United States and Canada. He's been interviewed and aired on many radio programs including the British Broadcasting System and has had countless articles written about his work in major newspapers and magazines throughout the world.

More information about this book and Paul M. Kramer's other books are available on his website at www.alohapublishers.com.